Teddy Rabbit

by Kathy Stinson

art by Stéphane Poulin

Annick Press Ltd.
Toronto, Ontario M2M 1H9

Second Printing, June 1988

Annick Press gratefully acknowledges
the contributions of the Canada Council
and the Ontario Arts Council

Design and graphic realization by Lise Monette

Canadian Cataloguing in Publication Data

Stinson, Kathy.
  Teddy Rabbit

ISBN 1-55037-017-0 (bound).—ISBN 1-55037-016-2 (pbk.)

I. Poulin, Stéphane.   II. Title.

PS8587.I56T42 1988   jC813′.54   C88-093818-8
PZ7.S74Te 1988

Distributed in Canada and the USA by:
Firefly Books Ltd.
3520 Pharmacy Avenue, Unit 1-C
Scarborough, Ontario
M1W 2T8

Printed and bound in Canada by:
D.W. Friesen & Sons, Altona, Manitoba

Dedicated with thanks to Dan,
for dropping his teddy bear
and to his father,
for telling me.

Tony and Rabbit went everywhere together.

When his mother said, "Don't take Rabbit to the library, Tony—he's too much trouble." Tony said, "Rabbit knows how to be very quiet."
When his mother said, "Don't take Rabbit to the market, Tony—the market is big, and he might get lost." Tony said, "But Rabbit likes to look at the vegetables. And he won't get lost. Rabbit never gets lost."

One morning at day care Tony said,
"We're going to the Teddy Bears' Picnic
on Saturday."

"You can't," said Andrew. "Rabbit's not a
teddy. He's a rabbit."
Tony hugged Rabbit tighter and said,
"Teddys don't have to be bears."
Quietly he added,
"Sometimes teddys are rabbits."
"Haven't you ever heard of a teddy rabbit,
Andrew?" asked Ms. Manning.
Tony smiled.
Andrew laughed. "No."
Tony frowned. He hoped Ms. Manning
was right. He hoped it would be okay to
take Teddy Rabbit to the
Teddy Bears' Picnic.

At night in bed Tony thought about the
Teddy Bears' Picnic.

He thought about all the children with
Teddy Bears shouting, "Go home, Rabbit.
This picnic is for Bears only."

But every morning Tony counted the days
till Saturday on the calendar.

Every day he
thought about the Teddy Bears' Picnic at
Centre Island, riding in the swan boats
with Teddy Rabbit, having lunch on the
beach or under a tree if Rabbit felt too hot.
He wondered if Rabbit would be afraid to
go on the skyride.

On Saturday Tony's dad came to take him
to Centre Island.
Tony's mom put some carrots in a bag,
even though Tony didn't much like them.
She tied Rabbit's blue and white checked
ribbon neatly around his neck.

Tony went with his dad down many
stairs, into the subway station.

They dropped their tickets into the box
and went down some more stairs.
Lots of people were on the platform
waiting for the train to come.
One of the people rushed past Tony
and knocked Teddy Rabbit
right out of his arms.

Tony saw Teddy Rabbit fall to the tracks far below
where it was dark and dirty, and dangerous.
He felt his dad grab him so he wouldn't
fall down, too.

"My Teddy," shouted Tony.
People on the platform gathered round.
"Poor boy, he's lost his teddy," said a big woman
with big flowers on her dress. She wiggled her hips
and shoulders and thought hard about what to do.
"Such a shame to lose a teddy," said a young man
with beads on his jacket. He stroked his beard and
thought hard about what to do.
"He looks a bit big to me to be worrying about a
teddy," said a sharp woman with long red
fingernails. She turned her pinched face away
from the crowd at the edge of the platform and
tapped her pointed foot.

"A teddy on the tracks you say?" said a woman in
a train station uniform. She radioed to the driver,
"Stop the train."
Then she rushed up the stairs.

Deep in the tunnel the train stopped. "There has
been an emergency in the next station,"
announced a voice over the loud speaker.
"There will be a slight delay in service."
People in the train frowned and shook their heads
and sighed.

"Can't somebody get my teddy?" cried Tony.
People on the platform frowned and shook their
heads and sighed.
A tear rolled down Tony's cheek.

Then the woman in the uniform ran back down
the stairs holding high a long black umbrella with
a curved wooden handle. "From the lost and
found," she explained. "Excuse me."

People made way for the woman with the umbrella.
The woman lay on her stomach and reached the
handle of the umbrella down into the dark, dark
space beside the platform.
She lifted the umbrella back up. Empty. She
stretched a little harder, reaching as far as she
could with the umbrella. The people on the
platform stretched, too.
Then, on the hook of the handle was Teddy
Rabbit, hanging by his blue and white checked ribbon.
The woman with the flowers wiggled and smiled.
The man with the beads stroked his beard and nodded.
The sharp lady with the fingernails sniffed.
The woman radioed to the driver of the train,
"Emergency situation all clear. You may proceed."

Tony scolded Teddy Rabbit for going on
the tracks.

When the train roared into the station,
Tony hugged Teddy Rabbit tight.
He hugged him tight on the subway train.
And waiting at the bus stop.
On the bus.
And waiting at the ferry dock.

On the ferry Tony looked through the railing at the fast water swishing past. He gave Teddy Rabbit an extra squeeze and sat right back on the bench.

Tony saw a girl beside him with a big bear tucked under her arm. Nearby stood a boy with a carriage full of teddy bears. He knew they must be going to the Teddy Bears' Picnic, too.

Tony looked at Teddy Rabbit sadly. He folded Rabbit's floppy ears behind his head but he knew he couldn't make a rabbit look like a bear. He didn't even want his rabbit to look like a bear. He just hoped rabbits were allowed at today's picnic.

"Tony, look," said his dad. He lifted Tony up. He was careful to put a hand around Rabbit, too. The ferry was docking at Centre Island.

On the Island Tony saw hundreds of children, and with the children were hundreds of teddy bears. Tony swallowed hard and hugged Rabbit against his sore tummy.

Then Tony saw that one of the teddy bears had a very long tail. It was not a bear. It was a monkey. "That's funny," Tony thought.
Then he saw that one of the teddy bears had a bushy mane of golden hair. It was not a bear. It was a lion.
Then Tony laughed. If Teddy Monkeys and Teddy Lions could come to the Teddy Bears' Picnic, he knew Teddy Rabbit would be welcome, too.

Tony and Teddy Rabbit sat at
a big table under a tree with
three Teddy Bears and two Teddy Cats,
with lots of sandwiches and cookies,
berries with honey, tinned tuna,
and of course,
carrots.